M000288715

Dear Parent:
Your child's love of re...

Every child learns to read in a different way and at his or her own speed. You can help your young reader improve and become more confident by encouraging his or her own interests and abilities. You can also guide your child's spiritual development by reading stories with biblical values and Bible stories, like I Can Read! books published by Zonderkidz. From books your child reads with you to the first books he or she reads alone, there are I Can Read! books for every stage of reading:

SHARED READING
Basic language, word repetition, and whimsical illustrations, ideal for sharing with your emergent reader.

BEGINNING READING
Short sentences, familiar words, and simple concepts for children eager to read on their own.

READING WITH HELP
Engaging stories, longer sentences, and language play for developing readers.

READING ALONE
Complex plots, challenging vocabulary, and high-interest topics for the independent reader.

ADVANCED READING
Short paragraphs, chapters, and exciting themes for the perfect bridge to chapter books.

I Can Read! books have introduced children to the joy of reading since 1957. Featuring award-winning authors and illustrators and a fabulous cast of beloved characters, I Can Read! books set the standard for beginning readers.

A lifetime of discovery begins with the magical words **"I Can Read!"**

Visit www.icanread.com for information on enriching your child's reading experience.
Visit www.zonderkidz.com for more Zonderkidz I Can Read! titles.

"The kingdom of heaven is like treasure that was hidden in a field."
—*Matthew 13:44*

ZONDERKIDZ

Princess Hope and the Hidden Treasure
Copyright © 2012 by Zonderkidz

Requests for information should be addressed to:

Zonderkidz, 5300 Patterson Ave. SE, Grand Rapids, Michigan 49530

ISBN 978-0-310-73250-1

Editor: Mary Hassinger
Design: Diane Mielke

Printed in China

12 13 14 15 16 17 /DSC/ 7 6 5 4 3 2 1

Princess Hope
and the Hidden Treasure

Story inspired by **Jeanna Young** & **Jacqueline Johnson**
Pictures by **Omar Aranda**

Princess Hope lived in a castle.

She had four sisters.

They are Joy, Faith, Charity,

and Grace.

Their daddy is the king!

Princess Hope is the oldest sister.

She loves her family and

her pet lamb, Lily.

She is kind, smart, and a good leader.

One day, Hope and her sisters

went shopping.

They went to their favorite shop.

There were pretty things

in the window.

There was something extra special

in the window!

Princess Hope went in the shop.

"May I see that ring, please?"

she asked the man.

"Yes, Princess," the man said.

"This was my grandmother's ring,"

Hope said.

"It was lost. May I buy it?"

But the ring cost too much.

Hope prayed, "Dear Lord,

help me come up with a plan."

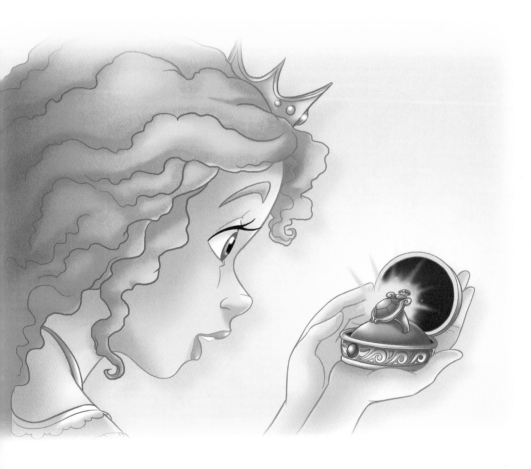

The princesses went back to the castle.

They talked about the ring.

Charity said, "Grandmother loved that ring."

Joy said, "It was from Grandfather."

Princess Hope said,

"Grandmother let me put it on my thumb."

All the princesses wanted to buy the ring.

Hope thought, *How will we get*

it back, Lord?

The princesses checked their

piggy banks.

"We do not have enough money,"

said Charity.

"What will we do?" asked Faith.

Hope had a plan.

She said, "Let's have a sale!

I will sell all of my things.

We will get the money."

The princesses had a sale.

Many people came.

People bought books and dolls.

They were all happy.

Hope and her sisters

were happy too.

They had money to get

Grandmother's ring back.

"We did it!" said Hope.

The princesses bought the ring.

"There is writing on the ring.

It says, 'Look behind the Royal Chart.'

That is our family tree," said Hope.

"There is a little door here," said Hope.

"And a box," said Faith.

"What is inside?" whispered Joy.

Hope opened the box.

There was a note in the box.

Hope read the note,

"'In the West Wing to be found,

the door is buried underground.'

The pantry is in the West Wing.

Let's go!"

"In the West Wing to be found, the door is buried underground."

The princesses looked and looked.

They found a trap door in the floor.

Hope found another note.

She read the note,

"'Under the stairs, and behind,

a loose stone you will find.'"

All the sisters helped look in

the stair closet.

They found a loose stone.

Hope moved the stone.

A secret door opened.

The princesses went into a little room.

They found a gold chest and a note.

Hope read the note out loud,

"'Use the ring, a treasure to bring.'"

Hope put the ring in the lock.

POP! The lock opened.

The girls opened the chest.

All of their grandmother's treasures

were in the chest.

It was filled with happy memories.

The princesses told the king

all about the ring and the sale.

They told him about the hunt.

They showed Grandmother's treasures

to their daddy too.

Later, the king tucked Hope into bed.

"Grandmother would be happy

you found the ring and her treasures.

I am proud you worked so hard

to get it all.

God bless you, daughter," said the king.